GINGER BEAR

MINI GREY

Alfred A. Knopf

New York

Our story starts with
a lump of pastry that
Horace's Mum gave him,

which Horace would usually roll about over the floor and furniture

until

it was

deep gray

and **fluffy**

(and quite a lot smaller).

But today

Horace's Mum gave him
a cookie cutter in the shape of
a bear to use.

Horace stamped out a gingerbread bear
and gave it currant eyes and a nose.

Horace's Mum put it in the oven to bake.

Twenty minutes later, the cookie bear was golden-colored and smelled lovely, and Horace wanted to take a bite, but–

"No, Horace," said Horace's Mum, "it is too hot. You must wait for it to cool down."

An hour later, Horace remembered the cooled gingerbread bear and was about to take a bite, but–

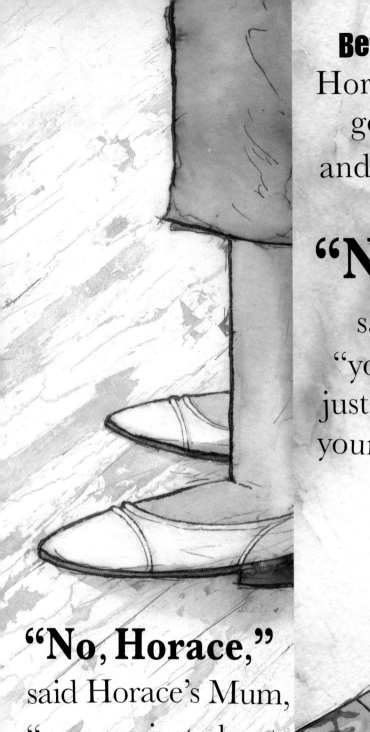

Before bedtime, Horace thought of the golden cookie bear and he was just gazing at it, but–

"No, Horace," said Horace's Mum, "you have just cleaned your teeth."

"No, Horace," said Horace's Mum, "you are just about to have dinner. You will spoil your appetite."

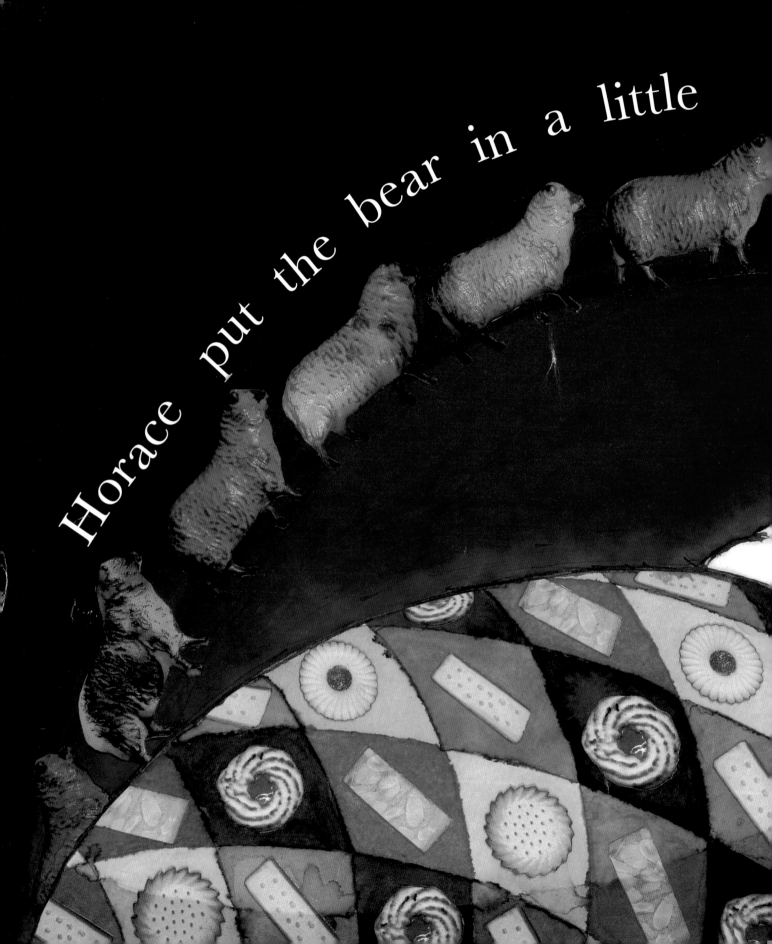

Horace put the bear in a little

tin and put it on his pillow.

It was the
middle of the night.
Ginger Bear woke up.
He yawned and stretched,
and looked about for
somebody to play with.
Everyone seemed
to be asleep.

Ginger Bear had an idea.
I shall **make** some friends,
he said to himself,
and went to the **kitchen**.

Ginger Bear found

butter and **flour** and **milk.**

He mixed up a mixture and rolled it and shaped it,

and put the first batch of friends in the oven to bake.

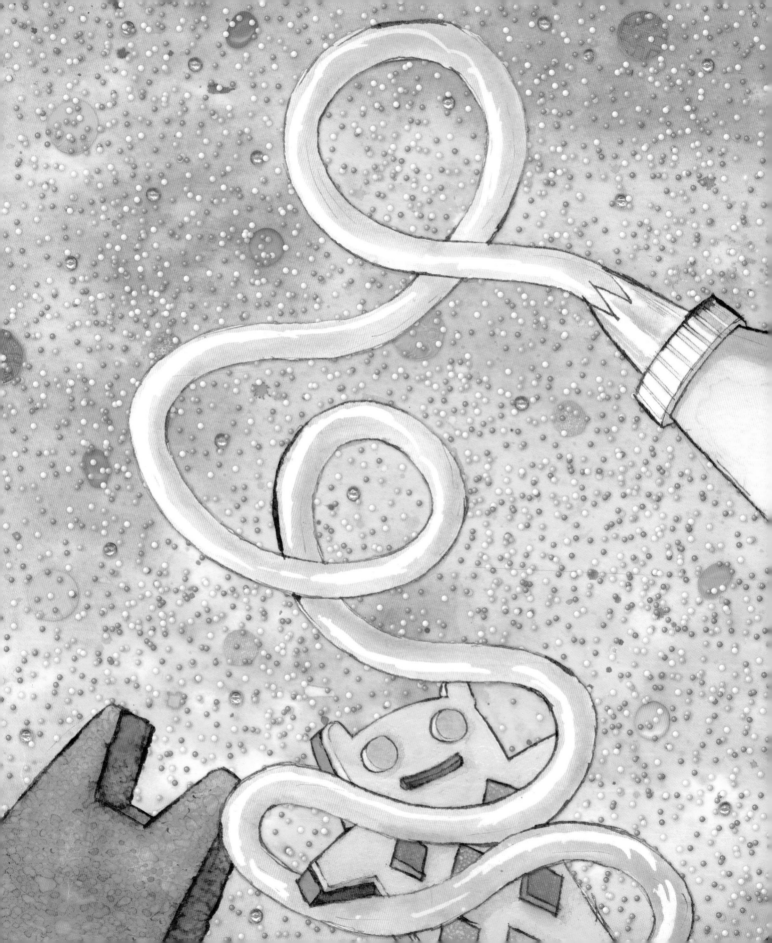

When they had cooled,
Ginger Bear dressed them in
icing of many colors,
thousands of sugar sprinkles,
and **candied peels** and *glacé* cherries
and little silver balls.

"And now,"
Ginger Bear said
to his new friends,
"let the fun begin!"

Come One!
Come All!

One night only!

Ginger Bear's Circus is performing in the kitchen!

Watch the Acrobats as they toss and tumble!

Gasp as Strongbear raises the rolling pin!

Scream with surprise as our Aeronaut is fired from the ketchup bottle!

The circus was so exciting
that no one noticed
the **shadow** looming
in the doorway.

Bongo the Dog liked cookies.
(But not in a way that is
necessarily good
for the
cookies.)

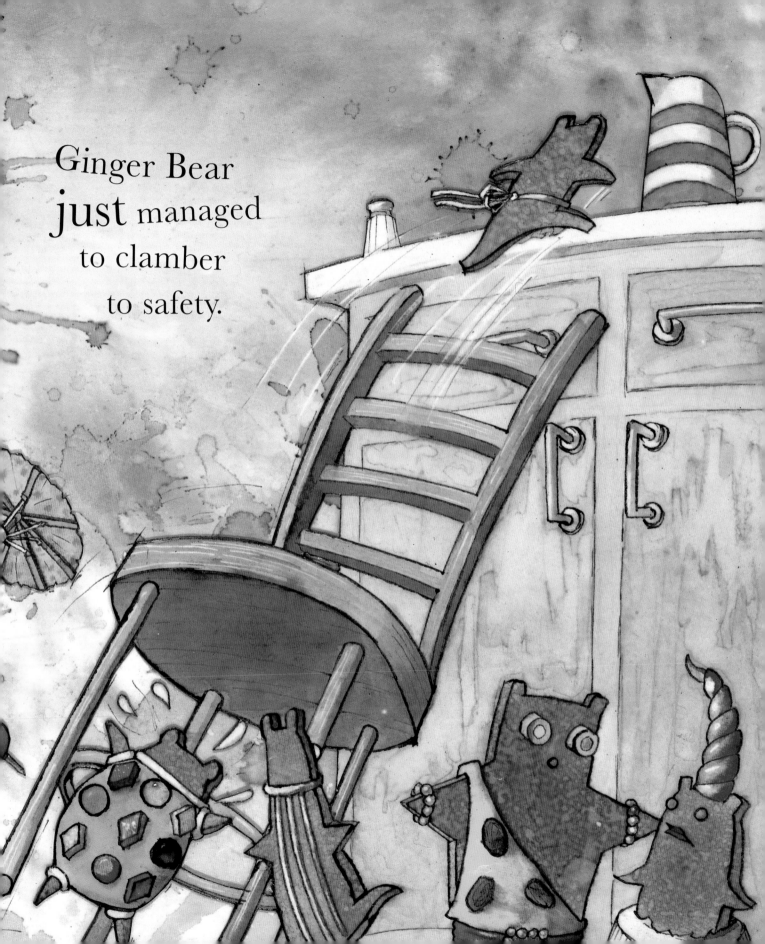

Ginger Bear **just** managed to clamber to safety.

Ginger Bear looked sadly at the mess.
He suddenly realized
that he needed to find
a place where a cookie
could be safe.

When Horace awoke the **next morning,**
he reached for the tin
that had contained the little cookie bear,

Horace

but all he found was crumbs
and a card
that looked
familiar.

The life of a cookie
is usually **short** and *sweet*,
but Ginger Bear has found
somewhere safe to be.

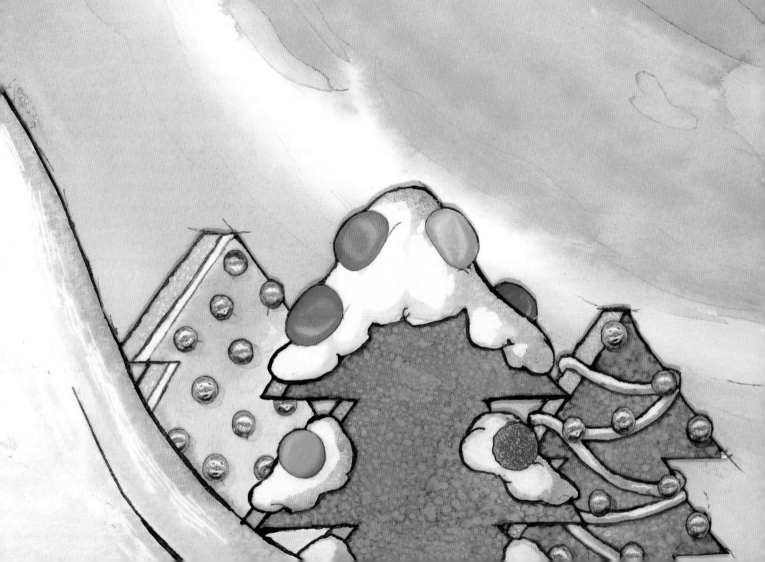

Ginger Bear is in
the pastry-shop display.
Some of it is cardboard,
covered in icing;
some of it is plaster.

It looks delicious,

but it can never be eaten.

The display changes
through the
year—

but every day

Ginger Bear is the **star.**
And every night . . .
who knows?

Dedicated to

Jo

(and to cookie lovers everywhere)

THIS IS A BORZOI BOOK PUBLISHED BY ALFRED A. KNOPF

Copyright © 2004 by Mini Grey

Published in the United States by Alfred A. Knopf, an imprint of Random House Children's Books, a division of Random House,
Inc., New York. Originally published in Great Britain by Jonathan Cape, an imprint of Random House Children's Books, in 2004.

KNOPF, BORZOI BOOKS, and the colophon are registered trademarks of Random House, Inc.

www.randomhouse.com/kids

Educators and librarians, for a variety of teaching tools, visit us at www.randomhouse.com/teachers

Library of Congress Cataloging-in-Publication Data
Grey, Mini.
[Biscuit Bear]
Ginger Bear / Mini Grey. — 1st American ed.
p. cm.
"Originally published in Great Britain by Jonathan Cape, an imprint of Random House Children's Books, in 2004" — T.p. verso.
SUMMARY: After a lonely gingerbread bear creates some friends by mixing up a new batch of dough, he realizes that being a cookie
has some major disadvantages.
ISBN 978-0-375-84253-5 (trade) — ISBN 978-0-375-94253-2 (lib. bdg.)
[1. Cookies—Fiction.] I. Title.
PZ7.G873Gi 2007   [E]—dc22   2006012240

The illustrations in this book were created using ink and Dr. Ph. Martin's Radiant Watercolors, plus some acrylic paint, collaged
pictures/photographs, and wood glue. No cookies were harmed in the making of the pictures.

MANUFACTURED IN MALAYSIA

June 2007

10 9 8 7 6 5 4 3 2 1

First American Edition

E
GRE

Grey, Mini.

Ginger Bear.

$18.99

39545000528850

DATE			